What This Book Does

Our series of translations introduces English-speaking children in India to children's literature in Indian languages.

Four Heroes and a Green Beard is the first English translation of *Jhowbunglar Rahasya*, a Bengali children's classic.

Bengali has one of the best traditions of children's writing, going back to the late nineteenth century. It is vibrant and humorous, consisting of detective fiction, nonsense verse, ghost stories, fantasy and science fiction.

Narayan Gangopadhyay's absurd and imaginative writing has delighted generations of Bengali readers, and his creation Tenida is one of the best known characters in children's fiction.

In *Four Heroes and a Green Beard*, Gangopadhyay parodies the Bengali mystery novel, making fun of its blood-curdling descriptions, strange characters and improbable plots.

Four Heroes and a Green Beard

©Narayan Gangopadhyay

English Translation © 1999 Tara Publishing

Translation: Swati Bhattacharjee
Design: Rathna Ramanathan
Photographs: Sirish Rao
Production: C.Arumugam

Tara Publishing
20 G/A Shoreham
5th Avenue, Besant Nagar
Chennai 600 090, India
Phone: +91 - 44 - 4903318
Fax: +91 - 44 - 4911788
 e-mail: tara@vsnl.com

Printed at The Ind-com Press, Chennai
ISBN: 81 - 86211 - 52 - 7

4 HEROES & A GREEN BEARD

Narayan Gangopadhyay

TARA PUBLISHING

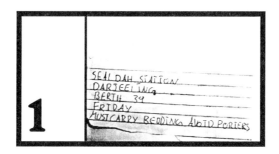

WHO IS SRI JHUMURLAL CHOUBE CHAKRABARTY?

It was all fixed. The four of us—Teni, Habul Sen, Kyabla and I, Pyalaram—would be going to Darjeeling in the summer vacation.

In Calcutta, the heat was terrific—nearly 107 degrees Farenheit. In the afternoons, the tar on the roads stuck to the car tyres. The wind was like fire. Even the quiet street dogs of our Patoldanga had become crazy with the heat. I threw a mango seed at one, and it actually bared its teeth at me! It did not even sniff the seed, let alone lick it.

Who could stay in Calcutta after this?

All four of us were first year undergraduate students at City College. We were not children any more, so it was not too difficult to get permission from our families.

Only my middle brother would not leave me alone. He had

just become a doctor, so he was itching to apply his knowledge on someone. To him, I was a walking hospital—a depot of all diseases on earth. If he could give me an injection every hour of the day, he would be happy.

"Go if you want," he said, "but be very careful! You lose your head at the sight of food, be it peanuts or chicken cutlet. And if you ever drink the water that comes to Darjeeling from Sinchal lake, you'll surely die of hill diarrhoea."

How does one reply to this? I didn't. I just sat with a long face.

But that was not all. My parents poured pots of advice on me, my elder brother issued warnings ("Don't try to stay on for one month, forgetting all about your studies"), my sister kept reminding me of her order: three dozen gold stones, six stone necklaces, six wall plates.

Somehow I said goodbye, reached Sealdah station and heaved a sigh of relief. The other three were already there, sitting in a third-class compartment. I didn't have to look for them.

Teni's loud voice boomed, "Come on Pyala, this way ..."

They were sipping orange squash.

I entered the compartment, dumped my bags and bedding and said, "What about my orange squash?"

"Yours has been cancelled. Fine for coming late," said Habul.

I screeched in protest. "What do you mean, late? The train won't start for another twenty minutes."

"What if the train had started twenty minutes early?" asked Teni in a sombre voice.

"How can it start twenty minutes early? The timetable ..."

"The timetable? Ha!" said Teni. "That's nothing but a joke book of the railways. Why, the day before yesterday my aunt came from Haridwar by Doon express. The timetable said the train was to arrive at five in the morning. It came at twelve noon. If it can come seven hours late, can't it start twenty minutes early?"

"What nonsense," I fumed. "I am going to have an orange squash too."

"Sure?"

"Yes."

"With your own money?"

"Of course."

"Who can stop you, Pyala?" said Kyabla. "Go ahead, get the orange squash. No, not one, four. We are all with you."

"I wholeheartedly support this proposal," quipped Habul.

"Ditto," said Teni.

They wouldn't let me off. I had to buy orange squash for everybody. But before we could finish, the bell went 'ting-ting-ting', and the North Bengal Express started.

I don't want to describe the route. Those of you who have been to Darjeeling know it only too well. It gallops through Sakrigali, hurries through Manihari and rushes on like mad.

Kyabla fell and rolled on the floor like a pumpkin, a pot of yoghurt hit Habul on the head, I twisted my left ankle, and Teni almost started a fight with a sly-looking man while changing to the narrow-gauge train.

We left all these small incidents behind and reached Siliguri in the morning. The Himalaya looked like a blue line in the horizon, white clouds floating on it. Outside the station, there was a crowd of buses and taxis.

"Darjeeling, Darjeeling, Kalimpong, Kalimpong ..."

The sly-looking man who had almost started a fight with Teni at Manihari was sitting in a bus, looking at us. Even in the heat of Siliguri, he wore a thick blue coat and a worn brown muffler. It was infuriating—the way he smiled beneath his thin moustache.

He stretched his neck and said, "Hey boys, going to Darjeeling?"

One should ignore people like him.

But Teni was bristling since the near-fight. He shouted, "We don't want to go anywhere with you."

What a shameless man! He now bared all his teeth in a grin. His teeth were betel-stained, two of them worn to stubs. "Why not? There are many seats left here. Come on."

"No."

He screwed up his eyes and showed more of his stained teeth.

"Still angry? Come, come, there are always arguments while getting into a train. One should not mind that. You are like my younger brothers. I can even tweak your ears in fun, if I want to. Come with me, I will show you the scenery on the way."

What cheek! He wanted to box our ears!

If the man hadn't been sitting in the bus, Teni would have

surely started a fight then and there. Now he could only shout, "Shut up!"

The man laughed aloud. "So you are not coming with me? Alas, you don't know what you are missing."

"We don't want to know."

The bus blew its horn and started.

The man put out his neck and said, "Here is a piece of chocolate for you. Perhaps you will need to think of me later. Then you won't be so angry with me."

He threw something at us and Kyabla, the wicket-keeper of Patoldanga club, caught it.

What a chocolate! It was a jumbo-sized one.

"Should I throw it away, Tenida?" asked Kyabla.

Teni never made mistakes about food, not even when he was angry. He snatched the chocolate from Kyabla's hands.

"Throw away a chocolate of this size? Who do you think you are, Nawab Siraj-ud-Daula?" he said. "This is mine. I fought with that man."

"Can't we have our share?" asked Habul.

Teni became serious. "That will be considered later," he said, and put the chocolate in his pocket.

The owners of buses and taxis kept calling, "Darjeeling, Darjeeling, Kalimpong, Kalimpong."

"What are we waiting for, Tenida?" I said. "Let's get into a bus."

"Wait, can't you?" he replied. "Let's eat first—at Sorabji's restaurant. We have to go fifty miles on a hilly road. If I don't eat now, my intestines will surely digest themselves."

So we ate first and then fixed a taxi. We opened our bags, took out warm clothes, and started on our way to Darjeeling.

Our car ran towards the bluish mountains. The road was beautiful. First we came across tea gardens, then the *sal* forests started on both sides. The cool wind felt wonderful on our bodies. Music welled up inside me.

Here I was born, and here I want to die, I sang.

Habul Sen put his hands over his ears. "What a tune, Pyala. You've ruined the famous song."

How dare Habul criticise my song? All he could get out of himself by way of music was a braying sound. I was furious.

"Who do you think you are Habul? An *ustad*?"

"Don't fight," Kyabla chipped in. "The point is, Pyala has no right to sing this song here. He can die here if he wants, even if we don't want him to. But he certainly was not born here. If he was, he would now be jumping from tree to tree, not travelling in this car with us."

What was Kyabla trying to say? Was he calling me a monkey? We did see some a few minutes ago.

I was about to say something when Teni suddenly gave out a shout.

"What does this mean? What can be the meaning of this poem?"

"Poem? What poem?"

Teni was holding a small piece of blue paper.

"Where did you get that from?"

"It was folded and tucked inside the packet of chocolate," said Teni. Habul took the paper from his hand and read aloud:

WHOEVER TO DARJEELING GOES

CAN SEE ONLY HORNED HIPPOS

BETTER GO TO BLUE HILLS

WHERE GREEN BEARD BRISTLES

THERE, IN JHOW BUNGALOW

THOUGH NOT IN 'WIND IN THE WILLOWS'

BABBLERS SING IN CHORUS

MR. KUNDU MAKES HEADS DANCE

- SRI JHUMURLAL CHOUBE CHAKRABARTY

The four of us were speechless.

"What does it mean?" asked Kyabla after five minutes, scratching his head.

The shadowy sal forests on both sides of the road could offer no answer.

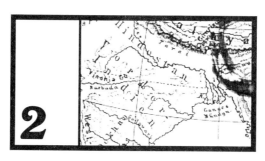

GREEN BEARD
OF BLUE HILLS

Once in Darjeeling, we forgot everything that had happened.

Who could think of anything else in Darjeeling except the Kanchenjunga range which fills up the whole sky, and the horses which trot in the Mall?

We climbed the hills and heard birds singing in the forests of Sinchal. While people in Calcutta were dying of heat stroke, licking ice cream to keep off their misery, we were shivering with cold even after putting on our coats.

We were lodged at the Sanatorium, the best place in Darjeeling to have fun. We did have some difficulty climbing up and down the hill, but the place was wonderful. It had a garden full of flowers, a lawn big enough for football or cricket, table tennis and carrom boards in the library. We ate our fill, roamed about, played games, took rides and snapped pictures.

After four or five days, Kyabla began to complain.

"I am getting bored." He appeared peevish.

"What do you mean?" The rest of us cried together.

"I mean I am bored."

Teni was furious. "Oh, he is missing his classes. Why don't you go to the colleges here? Go on, get into a logic class tomorrow."

We were munching something, sitting on a bench in the Mall. Kyabla leapt up.

"Okay then, I am going to rent a car. Tomorrow morning, I'll go to see the sunrise from Tiger Hill. All by myself."

Teni stretched out a long arm and caught Kyabla.

"Tiger Hill is another question. We will come too."

"No, you don't have to come. I'll go alone."

"Children should never go anywhere alone Kyabla," said Habul. "The tigers of Tiger Hill will eat you up."

"There are no tigers on Tiger Hill," said Kyabla with a glum face.

"Okay," I said. "If you insist on going alone, you can pay for the car. We will come as your bodyguards."

Kyabla threw up his hands.

"All you people ever do is talk. If you really want to go, come right now to fix a car. The weather has been nice the last few days. If it gets cloudy or foggy, we won't be able to see a thing."

Next day we started for Tiger Hill at four in the morning.

The whole of Darjeeling was frozen in the cold. We were in a jeep with no roof. The icy wind nearly tore away our noses and ears. The cold left us half-dead.

"Stupid Tiger Hill," said Teni. "This boy Kyabla will be the end of us. I'm freezing."

"Soon, we will be ice cream," added Habul.

"If comfort is all you want, why didn't you stay in Calcutta? Thousands of tourists come from all over the world to see the sunrise from Tiger Hill. And you are dying of a little cold," retorted Kyabla.

"Oh, a little cold, is it?" said Teni, his teeth chattering. "This is not cold enough for you? Okay then, I will douse you in a bucket of icy cold water tomorrow at midnight."

I had a suggestion. "The best way to warm up is to sing. Let's start a song in chorus."

Teni muttered something under his breath. Kyabla was quiet. But Habul was game.

The two of us started singing at the top of our voices, *Hey ho, row the boat, hey ho ...*

Our Nepali driver jumped up and let out a scream.

"Please don't startle me by shouting like that. Do you want an accident on this steep hilly road?"

What a bonehead!

"Right. Was that a song? That was a duet by a couple of jackals," Teni added.

Kyabla began to smile. I felt too miserable to say anything.

"Don't get upset, Pyala," Habul whispered in my ear. "What

do these people know of music? Tomorrow, the two of us will go to Birch Hill and sing in quiet."

At Tiger Hill, we found rows of cars and crowds of men. The two-storey building from where one could watch the sunrise was crowded. We found a little corner for ourselves on the first floor.

We all stared at the dark, black hill in front of us. The sun would rise from behind it, then spread its magic on Kanchenjunga on its left. Rows of cameras waited. Wisps of fog went up from the hills and the forests.

Then the sun rose.

It is no use describing the play of colours on the clouds and the mountains. Those of you who have seen the sunrise from Tiger Hill know it well. Those who haven't seen it will never know it.

Click! click! click! Cameras clicked on all sides.

We heard only exclamations: "Wonderful! Extraordinary! Unique!"

"Really, we can forgive Kyabla," said Teni. "I have never seen such a grand view."

Just then, a throaty voice spoke up beside us.

"Haven't you? If you want to see a better view, you should go to Blue Hills."

Blue Hills! The four of us jumped together. The rhyme came back to us.

The man who spoke was wrapped all over in a large blanket, with only his nose showing.

He spoke again in his throaty voice:

BABBLERS SING IN CHORUS

MR. KUNDU MAKES HEAD DANCE

Then he drew back his blanket and we could see his worn, brownish muffler and a sly smile on a foxy face.

"Who? Who's that?" cried Teni.

But the man just disappeared into the crowd.

We searched for him on the first floor, the ground floor, in the tea stall, even amongst the cars standing outside. He was nowhere to be found. It was as if he had emerged out of the fog and vanished into it.

The sun climbed up higher in the sky. Its rays lit up everything around us and Kanchenjunga shone golden in the sunlight. One after the other, the cars started towards Darjeeling. Where could he have gone?

"Strange," said Teni.

"Like a mystery story, isn't it?" I said. "Even more mysterious than Sherlock Holmes."

Habul Sen scratched his ears. "I have a feeling all this is the work of a ghost."

Kyabla was the coolest among us.

In Jhanto Hills, too, I had found that he never got flustered. He now said, "Whether he is a ghost or a mad man, he won't be able to cut much ice with us. Let's go and have some tea."

We had tea and then went to see Keventer's dairy. As soon

as I saw those large cows and fat pigs, I had this deep urge to do some research.

The pig, I felt, was a cousin of the mole. If one could cut off a bit from a mole's tail and feed it vitamins, it would surely turn to a pig! I often thought of asking my doctor brother about it.

Then we went to see Sinchal lake. But we were disappointed. It was not a lake like Chilka. Sinchal lake consisted of two large reservoirs. Water from the mountains was stored there and then transported to Darjeeling through pipes.

The place was nice, though. There were trees all around. It was very quiet.

My three friends went to see how the water was being pumped up. I sat down on a seat. This was my chance to finish the song which was so rudely interrupted in the morning.

I cleared my voice and began, as loud as I could get:

The wind is blowing hard,

The sky is getting dark,

O boatman, row your boat ...

"Bravo!" said someone from behind me,

I turned around. It was an old gentleman. He wore a monkey cap and a pair of blue sunglasses, sported a white moustache and carried a heavy stick. He must have come from a pathway between the trees.

"How well you sing," he said. "You do have originality."

What he meant was—though the song was written and set to tune by Rabindranath Tagore—I was singing it my own way.

I could not decide whether I should be furious or pleased.

"I need talented young boys like you. Will you come with me?" he said.

"Where?" I asked, taken by surprise.

The old man smiled. "Blue Hills."

Blue Hills again! I nearly choked.

He smiled again and said, "What can you see in Darjeeling? Nothing. Only crowds. You can maybe wander in the Mall without a thing to do, or ride a horse without reason, or visit Tiger Hill, shivering in the cold. Come to Blue Hills, where I stay. What a wonderful place it is. It's full of flowers. I stay in Jhow Bungalow."

Jhow Bungalow?

I choked once again.

Then the old gentleman pulled off his monkey cap. It revealed his beard. And I saw ...

I saw the colour of his beard.

It was green. Dark green.

I opened my mouth once, then shut it.

My head went round and round, like a spinning top.

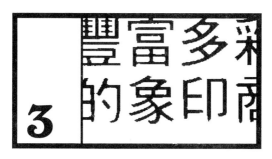

FORMULA
VS. KAGAMACHI

My head spun like a top, and I felt that all the trees in Sinchal hills had turned into one flowing green beard. The beard was going round and round.

I had stood up, but now I flopped down on the bench.

"What is the matter with you, my child?" The old gentleman's voice was kind.

I could only reply, "Oh, my God."

He started fussing around me. "What is it? Are you having stomach cramps? A muscle pull? Or do you have hysteria? You are too young for all these diseases, surely?"

My head cleared slowly.

I was about to say something when Teni, Kyabla and Habul returned.

Habul took one look at the old man, shouted "I'm gone!" and leapt back two feet.

Kyabla's eyes became the size of vegetable chops.

"De la Grande Mephistopheles," Teni pronounced.

The old gentleman frowned and looked at all of us.

"What is the matter?" he said. "Why are all of you so scared? And what was that you said? De la Mephistopheles?"

"That's French," said Teni.

"French?" He stroked his green beard thoughtfully. "I was in France for ten years. I have never heard such French. And Mephistopheles means Satan. Are you insulting me, an old man?"

Kyabla, the smartest among us, went up to him. "Actually, it is your beard."

"What about my beard?"

"None of us have ever seen a green beard on anyone, so ..."

"Oh, is that all?" The old gentleman laughed loudly.

We could see that one tooth in the front row was missing. Another tooth was gold. When he laughed, his nose made a peculiar noise.

We felt we could not take the gap in his teeth and the glitter of the gold tooth anymore. But thankfully, he stopped laughing.

"That's a whim of mine. I am a nature-lover. I spend my days engrossed in the trees. I have even written a book on them. So, to go with green nature, I have dyed my beard green," he explained.

"Sir, do you write poems?" asked Teni, somewhat suddenly.

His face brightened immediately.

"Poetry? Oh yes, I used to write poetry at one time. But that was long ago, you people were not even born then. Many of my poems came out in magazines. Now I have stopped writing poems. But sometimes, when the mood overwhelms me, poetry flows from inside me. Why, only the other night, I was writing an article. The moon was out, the tops of the pine trees were glistening in the moonlight. Suddenly, something happened. I found my pen pouring out poetry on its own. Listen to what I wrote:

IN THE BRIGHT

MOONLIT NIGHT

STANDS THE PINE

ISN'T IT LOOKING

ISN'T IT LOOKING

ISN'T IT LOOKING

FINE!

GENTLY FLOWS THE STREAM

STIRRING MY DREAM

MY THOUGHTS JOSTLE AND SCREAM

BREAKING ALL RULES OF RHYME

O PINE!

How do you like it?"

"Fine, fine," we all chorused.

He stroked his beard again and looked thoughtful. Maybe he wanted to recite another poem.

But Kyabla broke the silence.

"Can you make heads dance?"

"What do you mean? Whose head should I make dance?"

"Are you Mr. Kundu?" This was Teni.

"Kundu? Of course not. There is no Kundu in my entire clan. I am Sevenpenny Santra. My father was Fivepenny Santra. My grandfather was ..."

"Threepenny Santra," quipped Habul.

Sevenpenny was surprised. "How did you know?"

"That's easy, you were taking off two each time. Your great grandfather must have been Onepenny Santra. But I'm not sure what his father was called. Perhaps we should add a minus to his name?"

"Bravo, bravo!" Sevenpenny Santra patted Habul's back. "You are a bright boy. Don't you worry about my great grandfather's father's name, for even I don't know what he was called. Anyway, I am really very happy to meet you all. I invite all four of you to visit Jhow Bungalow."

"Jhow Bungalow?"

My three friends were startled.

"That's what I was telling your friend here. Oh, what a place! Not crowded, noisy and dirty like Darjeeling. There you will find forests of pine and *deodar*. Rows of streams dance their way down through these woods. Wild flowers bloom on all sides—*sehnai*, forget-me-nots, rhododendron. And my bungalow stands amongst all the flowers."

Sevenpenny Santra spoke almost as if he was singing a lullaby. "If you stay there for three days, even you will start writing poetry."

"If we could only understand Jhumurlal Choube Chakrabarty's rhymes before that!"

"Who?" said Sevenpenny. "Jhumurlal Choube Chakrabarty? What a terrible name! Does anyone by that name write rhymes?"

"Yes Sir! And that too, on your Jhow Bungalow."

"What?"

"Yes. And he mentions your green beard, too."

"Really? I'll sue that man for defamation."

"But where will you get him?" asked Teni. "That sly-looking man appears and then disappears. He has also written that babblers sing in chorus in your bungalow."

Sevenpenny was furious. "Babblers? How can babblers come to Blue Hills? Oh, I have got it. I sing *bhajans* now and then. How dare he call that a babblers' chorus? I'll send that man to jail."

"He has also said that one Mr. Kundu makes heads dance there."

"All rubbish. There is no Kundu there, only I and my servant Kanchha. I don't like making my own head dance, and I don't think Kanchha does either."

"Not just that," said Kyabla. "He invited us to Jhow Bungalow long before we met you."

"That sly man invited all of you to my own house? He is a criminal, a cheat. I'll send him to the gallows."

"But how can you catch him?" Habul sounded puzzled.

Sevenpenny Santra looked very grave for a few minutes. Then suddenly he sat down on the bench.

"Hmm, I've got it," he said, in a voice choked with self-pity.

"What?" The four of us cried together.

"This is the work of Kadamba Pakrashi, my arch rival. When I used to write poems, he would send letters to the magazines criticising them. Now he has become a spy of the famous Japanese scientist, Kagamachi. He wants to steal my newly discovered formula. I can see a terrible time ahead for Jhow Bungalow. Thieves, robbers, murderers. Oh my God!"

The four of us shivered.

Habul let out a cry. I looked at Teni and found that his nose, high as a mountain, had begun to look like a half-eaten *samosa*. He scratched his head for a while.

"Thieves, robbers, murderers? That's very serious. Why don't you inform the police?"

"Police? Police in all the continents of the world have been trying to get hold of Kagamachi for ten years but have not been able to touch a single hair of his. Not that he has any hair. He is totally bald. He is an expert in disguise. While in Calcutta, he is sometimes a Marwari businessman, sometimes a street hawker. He speaks all the languages of the world. Not just that. Once, when the police came looking for him, he hid in a thorny bush. They almost caught him that day. Then he started to bay like a mad jackal. The police were frightened. If he bit them, they would have surely contacted hydrophobia. So they escaped as fast as they could."

"So you're saying that the sly-looking man was Kagamachi?" I asked.

"No," he replied. "That was Kadamba Pakrashi. Did he have a moustache?"

"Yes," said Habul.

"And an old, brownish comforter around his neck?"

"That too."

"Then there can be no doubt. It was none other than that mother's eyesore, father's earache, that penniless parakeet, Kadamba Pakrashi."

"But why are they after you?" Teni wanted to know.

"Didn't you hear what he said?" Habul spoke up. "They are out to get his formula."

To Sevenpenny, he said, "You talk to Kyabla about formulas. He is the only one amongst us who is good at maths."

"Even you can understand my work," said Santra. "I was doing my research on trees and I have come up with a wonderful invention. I can raise a tree on which mango, jackfruit, apple and grape will grow together. And in all seasons."

"Really?" We gaped.

"That is why they have started this conspiracy against me." Sevenpenny Santra shook his head sadly. "Oh, what will happen to me?"

Still, everything was not clear to us yet. Kyabla looked a little suspicious.

"But if they wanted to steal your formula, wouldn't they try to do it quietly and secretly?" he asked. "Why should they drop rhymes on every street corner? That would only betray their plans."

"That's Kagamachi's style. He always creates an atmosphere of mystery before he starts working." Sevenpenny Santra nearly started weeping. "Will you not save me in this crisis? You, the young men of today. Won't you stand by my side?"

He said this in such a sorry tone that I felt my insides melting.

"Of course we will," said Teni.

"Promise?"

"Promise."

"I'm relieved," said Sevenpenny Santra and got up. "I'll meet you at four-thirty this evening, in the park above the Natural Museum."

No sooner were the words out, than he disappeared into the forest like a squirrel—green beard, stick, overcoat and all.

Just like that sly rascal, Kadamba Pakrashi.

4

CHOCOLATE
NUMBER 2

When Sevenpenny Santra—with his green beard, blue sunglasses, monkey cap and huge overcoat—disappeared into the forests of Sinchal, we stared at each other open-mouthed, like the crows of Calcutta.

It was Habul Sen who first moved, but only because a bumble bee was targeting his left ear. He danced a few steps to chase away the bee.

Then he turned to Teni and asked, "What was that all about, Tenida?"

Whenever Teni is thoughtful, he starts speaking French.

"De-Lux," he now said.

"What does that mean?" I asked.

"Poondicherry," said Teni. French again.

"Do you mean Pondicherry?" asked Kyabla. "What does

Pondicherry have to do with this?"

Teni bared his teeth in irritation.

"Shut up, Kyabla. Don't try to show off. Poondicherry in French means, 'the situation is serious'."

"Of course not," said Kyabla. "My uncle used to practise medicine in Pondicherry. I know."

"You are sure you know?"

"Yes."

Khatang! Teni landed a rap on Kyabla's head.

Kyabla leapt back like a jumbo prawn.

"Say that again!" roared Teni.

"I have forgotten what I knew," said Kyabla, rubbing his head. "You are right. Poondicherry means the situation is extremely serious—and I feel now that it is dangerous too."

"All right!" Teni sounded pleased. "That scholarship in the school final exams has spoilt you, Kyabla. If you start talking again I'll give you one slap and your ears will fly off to ..."

"Ernakulam," said Habul.

"Correct," said Teni. "I always say Habul is my first assistant. Anyway, what should we do now? That green-bearded man has landed us in real trouble."

"We have promised to help." Kyabla reminded him.

"But what if that Japanese scientist, Kagamachi, pounces on us?"

"We will swat him like a fly!" I said heroically.

"You? You will do that, you?" mocked Teni. He turned to me,

screwed up his nose and made a face like a plate of mashed potatoes. "You, with a body like a tuna fish? Kagamachi and Kadamba Pakrashi will make fish fry out of you and eat you up with chips."

"Let's not talk any more about this," said Habul Sen. "We will be meeting the man in the evening. We can decide then. Now let's go back, I am hungry."

Teni was about to snap at him when we heard a shout.

What a shout!

Who was that?

Who else, but our driver? The same chap who had refused to listen to our song. He had become impatient, waiting for us.

"Do you want to spend the entire day in Sinchal?" He barked at us. "Then pay me off and let me return to Darjeeling."

"And how are we to return?" asked Teni.

"You can walk to Ghoom," he said, "and catch a train from there."

"We're coming!" I said.

The four of us went to the jeep and slumped into our seats. Sevenpenny Santra, his formula of the four-in-one plant, the Japanese scientist Kagamachi and that ragamuffin Kadamba Pakrashi—all these went round and round in our heads.

Meanwhile, our jeep spiralled down the hilly road. I was sitting next to the driver.

"Driver *sahib* ..." I began.

"I am not the driver. I am the owner of this car. My name is Bajra Bahadur."

"Okay. Bajra Bahadur Singh sahib ..."

"Not Singh. Thapa."

He certainly was not a timid man. No one could mistake him for one. His temper and voice saw to that.

I checked myself and asked, "Do you know Blue Hills?"

"Of course," said Bajra Bahadur. "It's very near Pubang. And Pubang is where I live."

Kyabla now became interested.

"Have you seen Jhow Bungalow there?" he asked.

"Oh yes. An old sahib called Mackenzie built it. When India became independent, he sold it off and went to Britain. Now a Bengali *babu* from Calcutta owns it."

"How is the bungalow?"

"Ramro chah," said Bajra Bahadur.

"Ramro chah?" Habul was puzzled. "Oh I see. Whoever goes there must say 'Ram Ram'."

"No, no." A ghost of a smile stole over Bajra Bahadur's stern face. "Ramro chah is Nepali. It means, 'Fine, it's a nice place.'"

"Who lives there now?" asked Kyabla.

"That I don't know."

"How will it be if we go there on a visit?"

"Ramro," said Bajra Bahadur. "You can come in my car. I will give you a concession. I will also arrange for pure milk and fresh butter from Pubang."

It was almost lunch time when we reached the Sanatorium.

After a hurried bath and lunch, we began our conference on the lawn outside.

Teni had brought around forty *litchis* with him—his dessert after lunch.

He threw one into his mouth and said, "Forget it. I am not getting into all this mess. We have come to Darjeeling for a few days. We will walk around, ride a little, put on a few pounds weight and go home."

"But we gave our word to the old gentleman only this morning," Kyabla reminded him.

Teni threw a litchi seed at a crow on a pine tree in front of him.

"And we can withdraw that word in the evening, can't we? Green beard, Kagamachi. All bogus."

"But Bajra Bahadur has promised fresh milk and butter from Pubang," I said.

Teni poked me in the stomach. "Your greed will be the end of you, Pyala. Do you want us to walk into the arms of Kagamachi? He will make cockroach chutney out of us."

And he threw another litchi into his mouth.

"You're right," said Habul, nodding his head gravely. "We should not invite trouble."

"Okay then," I said. "Even I find Sevenpenny Santra suspicious. Did you see how he disappeared among the trees?"

"I have a feeling he was a ghost," said Habul.

"What nonsense," cried Kyabla. "How can a ghost come to

Sinchal in the afternoon? Admit that you are cowards. All of you."

"What did you say? Coward?"

Teni was about to deliver a slap when a boy from the Sanatorium appeared. He had a small packet in his hand.

"Timiro lie," he said.

"What?" said Teni. "Why should we lie down in the afternoon?"

Kyabla laughed and said, "No, he means, 'for you'."

Teni opened the packet. It was a large chocolate.

"Who gave this to you?"

The boy told us in Nepali that he had gone to the market a little while ago. There he had met a man with a thin moustache and a brown muffler who gave him the packet and asked him to give it to the boys from Calcutta.

Thin moustache, brown muffler! Who else but ...

Teni opened the chocolate wrapper. A folded paper fell on the ground.

On it were the lines:

AREN'T YOU GOING TO BLUE HILLS?

TURNIP-HEADS, PUMPKIN PEELS!

IF YOU LET THIS FRIGHTEN YOU

GO BACK HOME AND GRASS YOU CHEW

Habul read out the poem to us.

"Kadamba Pakrashi!" the three of us shouted together.

For a little while, we were all quiet.

Teni looked grave. He held a litchi in front of his mouth but did not immediately pop it in. I had never seen Teni show such restraint before.

"What now, Tenida?" said Kyabla.

"Hmmm." The sound came from Teni's nose.

"He has called us overgrown fools. Advised us to go back and chew grass."

"Yes," said Habul. "The enemy has thrown us a challenge."

Kyabla spoke again. "Should we accept defeat and go back? And chew grass?"

"Never," Teni shouted. "We must go to Blue Hills!"

"Sure?"

"Sure." And he popped the litchi into his mouth.

My eyes were fixed on the chocolate.

"Should we then share Kadamba Pakrashi's chocolate and then ..."

"Shut up Pyala!" said Teni. He could be very precise when he wanted to.

At five, the four of us were at the park near the natural museum. Tourists thronged the Mall. The horses cantered towards Birch Hill.

We sat on a bench in the middle of the deserted park, waiting for Sevenpenny Santra. There was nobody else around.

Twenty minutes passed.

At our feet was a hillock—of peanut shells. No sign of Green Beard.

"Where is this Green Beard, Kyabla?" Teni was getting irritated.

"Didn't I tell you it was a ghost of the Sinchal hills?" said Habul. "He will never come here."

"Don't be so impatient," said Kyabla. "Let's wait a little more. I have a feeling he will come."

"And I have," said someone behind us.

We jumped and turned around.

Dusk had cast long shadows on the garden. Fog was coming down thick on all sides. It was as if the park was cut off from the rest of the world.

And there stood the old man in a monkey cap and dark glasses.

Teni was about to say something, but Sevenpenny put his finger on his lips.

"Shhh! Kagamachi's spies are on all sides. Let me say only what is absolutely necessary. You are coming to Blue Hills?"

"Yes."

"Tomorrow morning?"

"Tomorrow morning."

"Fine," he whispered. "It will take you about one and a half hours by taxi. You will be my guests. I will pay for the taxi too. Agreed?"

"Yes, agreed," said Habul.

"I'll be off, then. See you at Jhow Bungalow. But remember one thing. Crackers."

"Crackers?" I was surprised. "What do you mean?"

"Kagamachi's signal. Goodbye."

In a moment, he had vanished into the fog. We could not even make out which way he had gone.

Kyabla stood up. "Let's go, Tenida."

"Where?"

"To the taxi stand. We must find out Bajra Bahadur."

He had barely finished speaking when ...

A cracker whizzed past and just missed Habul's left ear before it landed on the grass.

It was of the type that dances around before it bursts. It spewed fire and danced in the grass, then burst and disappeared into a bush of forget-me-nots.

BHAUA TOADS
AT JHOW BUNGALOW

The four of us watched the dancing cracker, our mouths wide open. Long after it entered the bushes and fizzled out, we could not speak a word.

The park was absolutely empty.

A thick, white curtain of fog had screened out everything. Even the lights which had come up on all sides had been wiped out by the fog. It was as if the four of us were sitting in the middle of a spine-chilling mystery story.

Teni spoke up at last. "Hey, what was that?"

Habul tried to speak with a peanut in his mouth and nearly choked on it. He coughed for some time and said, "Easy enough! Kadamba Pakrashi is after us."

"Maybe Kagamachi himself set that cracker on us," I said.

"Just see what we have landed ourselves into," said Teni.

"Here we are, spending a nice summer vacation, and that ragamuffin, ragtag Kadamba Pakrashi comes after us. On top of that arrives the green-bearded Sevenpenny Santra and the Japanese scientist Kagamachi. I don't like all this, I tell you."

"Just our luck." Habul was upset. "Last time we went on a holiday to Jhanto Hills, and that terrible Swami Ghutghutananda came after us."

"What are you complaining about?" asked Kyabla. "Didn't we all get gold medals for turning that gang over to the police?"

Teni made a face which looked like a plate of *alu chaat.*

"Forget the gold medals," he said. "Ghutghutananda was at least a Bengali. We managed to tackle him. But these Japanese are dangerous. I have read about them in detective novels."

"Yes, yes, I have read about them too," said Habul, nodding his head. "They'll catch each of us, give us an injection, and we will lie flat on our backs like *Bhaua* toads. Then they will make a hole in our skulls and put monkey's brains into our heads."

"And then we will grow tails, jump onto treetops and munch on tender leaves," I added. "And our Tenida ..."

"Will be the leader of the gang, the Lord of the Monkeys!" said Habul.

Teni delivered an instant rap on Habul's head. "How dare you crack jokes with a respectable elder?" he roared. "And at a time when I am dying of tension? You Habul, what is a Bhaua toad?"

"A Bhaua toad is a Bhaua toad," replied Habul.

"Stop that, please!" Kyabla was annoyed. "Listen Tenida, I have a suspicion."

"What?"

"I have a feeling that the cracker was thrown by none other than the old gentleman."

That gave the three of us a start.

"What? How's that possible?"

"That's what I feel. He was fingering his pocket before he got up. I think I heard the rustle of a matchbox, too."

I said, "Then perhaps the old gentleman is ..."

"Kagamachi himself," said Habul.

Teni made a face like an omelette. "Don't be silly. If he is Kagamachi himself, why should he be so scared of Kagamachi? Or invite us to his bungalow?"

"Because he wants to give us injections and turn us into Bhaua toads," said Habul once again.

"What? Again?" Teni shouted. "If you can't tell me what a Bhaua toad is ..."

"A Bhaua toad is a Bhaua toad."

Teni stretched out a long hand to catch hold of Habul's ears when Habul gave a leap—like a Bhaua toad, perhaps.

Kyabla was getting very restless.

"Do you people want to sit here and talk all night? Won't you arrange a car to go to Jhow Bungalow?"

Teni looked crestfallen. "Must we go?"

"Of course," said Kyabla. "Kadamba Pakrashi has sent us a

second chocolate and mocked us, called us cowards. Are we to simply swallow all this and go back home? What about the prestige of our Patoldanga?"

"Of course we are going." Habul and I cried together.

"Get up, then. Let us go and fix up Bajra Bahadur's car. We must leave early tomorrow."

To tell you the truth, I could not sleep well that night. I did overeat a little at dinner and felt very uncomfortable all night.

I dreamt that a large black crow was sitting near my head, gulping flies one by one. Then he pecked me on my head and said in the voice of an old man, "Go to Blue Hills and see what I do to you."

I woke up, panting, and saw Habul Sen standing before me, flashing all his thirty-two teeth at me. In his hand was a pencil. It all looked very suspicious.

"What was that, Habul?" I asked.

"I came to wake you up," said Habul. "We are leaving for Blue Hills."

"But why strike on my head with a pencil? Is that a way to wake up anyone?"

Habul's teeth flashed another smile. "Can't you see I was doing an experiment?"

"What experiment?"

"I was trying to gauge the ratio of grey matter and cowdung inside your head."

What an awful boy!

I was furious. "Why don't you sound out your own head? You'll find cowdung—hundred percent."

"Why are you getting angry? Come, have some tea and cool down," said Habul.

We joined Teni and Kyabla at the breakfast table. I had hardly finished when Bajra Bahadur arrived with his car.

"Get up, Pyala," said Kyabla. "Don't sit here munching toast like a cow."

"You have cleaned out your plates," I complained. "When it comes to me ..."

"Who told you to sleep on till eight?" Teni let out a roar.

It was no use arguing, really. I got up with a few pieces of toast in my hand. I did not leave behind the *sandesh* either. I put them in my pocket.

"If I die in the hands of Kagamachi, at least I can eat sandesh before I meet my fate," I thought.

At last we set out on our adventure.

As soon as the car drove past Darjeeling railway station, Teni shouted: "Patoldanga ..."

"Zindabad," the three of us shouted in chorus, like jackals.

Bajra Bahadur turned his face from the steering and asked, "What Zindabad did you say?"

"Patoldanga," the four of us said.

"What is that?"

What a turnip! He had not heard of Patoldanga. Nor did he realise that the Four Heroes of Patoldanga were setting out for an adventure in his car.

Teni made a face like a plate of *upma*.

"Patoldanga is our motherland."

"No, no," Habul corrected him, "our mother-locality."

Kyabla added, "Or what you can call De la Grande Mephistopheles."

Bajra Bahadur stared at us, open-mouthed, for a few minutes. Then he muttered to himself and drove on.

I sat looking at the lovely view. The path wound its way up through the line of trees, sometimes going up, sometimes down. The trees, the flowers, the foaming, milk-white hill streams leaping down to deep crevices covered with fog ...

We left behind Ghoom, took the Peshk road and proceeded towards Tista.

I felt like breaking into a song again but remembered Bajra Bahadur's warning and checked myself.

He was a quick-tempered man, and had been put off by Kyabla's 'De la Grande Mephistopheles'. I didn't want to risk making him angry again. He had promised milk and butter from Pubang. Besides, the car was in his hands. If he got mad at the sound of my song and lurched the car a little to the left, we would surely go down the thousand-feet crevice.

Suddenly Kyabla spoke up.

"Tenida, what if we go there and find that the entire story is bogus?"

"What do you mean?"

"What if there is no one called Sevenpenny Santra at Jhow Bungalow? What if that green-bearded man was playing a joke on us?"

Teni didn't look too disappointed. In fact, he appeared to be quite pleased.

He said, "What a relief! We won't have to tackle that rascal Kagamachi, then."

"All this pain, for nothing," grumbled Habul.

"Why nothing?" Teni gave Bajra Bahadur a sideward glance. "Aren't we going to have butter from Pubang?"

The car took a turn to the right. On two sides stretched the pine forest, bushes of tiger fern, rows of sehnai flowers. The lane was narrow, shadowy and dark. Lots of butterflies were fluttering around. I have never seen so many butterflies together ever before.

We were at least twelve miles away from Darjeeling.

Bajra Bahadur turned around and said, "We have entered the Blue Hills area."

Blue Hills! The four of us shifted in our seats.

And just then, Kyabla shouted.

"Look, Tenida! Can you see what is written on that rock?"

I stretched out my neck and saw, written in big Bengali letters, the word 'Crackers.'

I looked at another rock. On it was written, 'Mr. Kundu'.

Habul shouted, "And here it is written, 'Babblers'."

Teni said, "Driver *sahib*, please stop the car for a minute."

Bajra Bahadur looked at him sternly. "I am not the driver. I am the owner."

"Yes, yes, okay. Please stop for a minute."

"In a minute," said Bajra Bahadur. He drove the car around another corner and slammed on the brake.

"Get down. This is Jhow Bungalow," he said.

We were taken aback. There was a hillock, a flight of steps went up its side. Where the steps ended, there stood a lovely bungalow surrounded by pines and flowering plants.

It looked like a picture from a foreign book.

Then we saw Sevenpenny Santra standing there—in an overcoat, monkey cap, blue sunglasses and a stick.

From inside the cap came a deep voice. "Welcome, welcome. I have been waiting for all of you for long."

Just then a gust of wind arose and something crackling flew on my face. I caught it and saw what it was.

A chocolate wrapper.

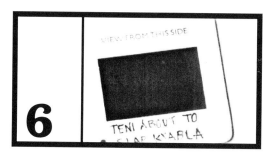

A FILM SHOW
AT MIDNIGHT

Bajra Bahadur left with his car for Pubang.

He assured us he would come the next day and take us wherever we wanted to go. Teni did not forget the important offer he had made.

"What about butter from Pubang?"

"Let us see," said Bajra Bahadur with a smile and left. Sevenpenny Santra had already paid him.

The four of us entered Jhow Bungalow. It really was a lovely place. Pine trees stood on all sides and the garden was full of flowers. There was even a stream that flowed merrily.

The inside of the bungalow was also cheerful. It had a huge drawing room with large sofas, lots of furniture and foreign paintings on the walls.

Sevenpenny took us around the two floors of the bungalow.

Then he showed us a large hall on the first floor. "This is where you sleep. Do you like the room?"

Did we like it? Of course we did!

There were four beds for the four of us, a dressing table and two wardrobes. On one side of the room stood a big dining table with four chairs. There were flowers in a vase on the table. There was an attached bathroom as well. On a bookshelf, there were a few English magazines. From the three windows on the three walls, we could see hills, forests and tea gardens.

"Can you see that tea garden?" said Sevenpenny. "It has a funny name. It's called 'Runglee Rungliot'."

What a name!

"What does that mean?" Teni was curious.

Habul shook his head wisely. "That's easy. Mother is calling her son, 'Hey Runglee, get up, it's time to have your oats.'"

Sevenpenny caressed his beard and smiled. "No, my boy. In the local language, 'Runglee Rungliot' means, 'this far and no further'."

"How strange. Why is it called that?" I asked.

"There is a story. I'll tell you later. Can you see that hill on the other side of the garden? That is Mongpu."

"Mongpu?" Kyabla cried out. "Isn't that where Rabindranath Tagore came to stay?"

"Right," smiled Sevenpenny. "That is why something happens to me whenever I look at that hill. Suppose I am writing a complicated scientific article. Suddenly I look up and see Mongpu and ..."

"And you start writing poetry?" said Habul.

"Of course. Poetry starts flowing from my pen."

I remembered the poem on the pine that he had recited in Sinchal.

"Pyala might be a problem, then." Teni butted in. "He is quite a poetry addict. He might just stay up at night writing poetry. Though he never gets more than twelve in maths, his poems are not too bad."

I didn't quite mind the poetry addiction part, but the mention of my maths mark put me off.

I snarled at Teni. "What about you, Tenida? Didn't you get seven-and-a-half in English?"

"You Pyala, shut up." Teni leapt towards me but was stopped by Sevenpenny.

"Please, please," he cried, "We don't want a civil war when the war with Kagamachi is still to be fought."

That awful Kagamachi again! I had almost forgotten all about him. The mention of his name did not improve my mood.

"Someone threw a cracker at us in the park, right after you left," said Teni.

"Really?" Sevenpenny gulped in surprise. "Then his spies must have been there. Must be Kadamba Pakrashi."

"On our way here, we saw 'Mr. Kundu' written on a rock," I added.

"And 'Babblers' at another place," said Habul.

"You don't need to say any more," sighed Sevenpenny. "The

enemy is now ready to spring upon me. There is no way I can save my formula from Kagamachi."

He held his head in his hands and let out a series of awful groans.

"Let us call the police, then," suggested Kyabla.

"Police?" Sevenpenny shook his head. "The police can't do a thing. My friends, you are my last hope. Won't you save me? Won't you help me?" Tears came to his eyes as he spoke.

My heart melted. I felt I could lay down my life for him.

Even Teni sounded sorry, "Don't worry Mr. Sevenpenny, we are with you," he said.

Habul was about to say something equally heroic when Kanchha, Sevenpenny's servant, came in and announced lunch.

Some good news at last. The bread and eggs we had in Darjeeling had been digested long ago. And, to tell you the truth, even amidst all that tension, the delicious smells from the kitchen distracted us, reminding us of other things.

The day went off well. Food was plentiful and we did justice to it. In the afternoon, Sevenpenny read out his poems.

He also spoke of his four-fruits-in-one-plant formula. I wanted to have a look at the formula. He drew his eyebrows into a dreadful frown and glared at me.

"Do you know what encyclopaedic catastrophe is?"

My God! Even Kyabla, the scholarship-winner in the school finals, looked a little lost.

"Have you ever opened the Prantoshini Mahaparinirban Tantra?"

Teni's voice sounded as if it had a mouse hidden in it. "We haven't," he squeaked, "and we don't want to."

"Do you know the combination of Nebuchadnazzer and positron?"

"No."

"Do you know what happens if you add Aqua Tycotis to the theory of relativity?"

"I'm gone," croaked Habul.

Sevenpenny smiled and said, "Then you won't understand anything by looking at the formula."

Kyabla scratched his head and thought for a while.

"Look," he said. "Aqua Tycotis is a digestive tonic, isn't it? How can you add Aqua Tycotis to the theory of relativity?"

"That is the mystery of my research." Sevenpenny smiled again. "If you understood that, you could have discovered the formula yourself."

"Of course, of course," said Teni. "Don't you listen to Kyabla. He has to say something on every occasion. Listen, Kyabla, if you try to show off again I'll give you one slap and your ears will fly to ..."

"Ernakulam," I finished.

"Please, don't fight among yourselves," said Sevenpenny. "Look, it's evening. Have your tea and go for a walk. We will talk again in the evening."

We went out.

It was a quiet place. The village had only a few people.

The forests were full of flowers and streams. The fog was

dense one moment and thin the next. We could see a part of the plain in the distance, where a silvery thread of a river shone in the afternoon sun. That was the Tista valley, a local man told us.

After the crowds and noise of Darjeeling, Blue Hills was a haven of peace. The more I saw the Mongpu hills, the more I thought that anyone could become a poet if he stayed here. If only that awful Kagamachi was not here ...

But where was Kagamachi? There was no sign of him anywhere. Then who wrote all those words on the rocks?

In the evening, we once again sat in the drawing room and talked idly. Sevenpenny read out to us a long poem he had written while we had gone for our walk.

Part of it went like this:

O MOUNTAINS, GREEN AND COOL

YOU LOOK SO BEAUTIFUL

YOU MAKE MY MIND DANCE LIKE WAVES

TILL I QUITE FORGET MYSELF

YOU'RE THE STOREHOUSE OF MY EMOTIONS

AND GIVE ME FOOD FOR THOUGHT

"You could write, 'food for my tummy,'" suggested Teni.

"I could," said Sevenpenny. "But you know, 'food for my tummy' doesn't sound nice in a poem."

"What about 'storehouse of grains'," wondered Habul, "instead of 'storehouse of emotions'?"

We spent the evening in intense intellectual activity.

Then after a huge dinner, we tucked ourselves nicely into our beds.

It was a new place, so it was a while before we slept. For a long time, we lay listening to the crickets outside and the stream in the distance.

"Look," said Kyabla suddenly. "I have serious doubts about Sevenpenny. Aqua Tycotis combined with the theory of relativity—is he joking? He says he is a scientist, but there is not a single book on science in this house. All I could see were a few foreign magazines and some detective novels. I have a feeling that ..."

Suddenly, Kyabla stopped.

"What is that sound?" he whispered.

Krrr ... came a sound from the room next to ours, as if someone had just started a machine. And then ...

A square of white light fell on the wall of our dark room.

What was that? The four of us sat up in our beds.

Pictures!

On the wall appeared our pictures—taken with a movie camera!

The four of us going around in the Mall, Teni about to slap Kyabla, our car coming to a halt at Jhow Bungalow.

Then, in bad handwriting appeared the words:

YOU'LL WATCH SEVERED HEADS DANCE

AND BABBLERS SING ALL AT ONCE

NOW STARTS KAGAMACHI'S TRICK

HE'LL MAKE YOU VANISH LIKE MAGIC

And, at the very last:

GET READY FOR A TERRIBLE MISHAP

- JHUMURLAL FOR KAGAMACHI

The square of white light went off.

The krrr ... sound also stopped.

"The next room," shouted Kyabla. "They are running a projector from there."

Teni put on the light.

Kyabla ran to the door of the next room and gave it a kick. It did not open.

Habul tried to open our bedroom door. That did not open either.

It appeared locked from outside.

7

THE DANCING HEAD

We pulled the door with all our might and shouted at the top of our voices. Nothing happened. The door did not budge even an inch.

At last, Habul gave up and flopped down on the floor.

"Now Kagamachi will come and pop us into his mouth, one by one," he wailed.

"Eat up all four of us? You must be joking," said Kyabla.

As usual, he was the only one who had not lost his cool.

"There is a large tree near the east window, Tenida. We can climb down that tree if we want."

Outside, the night was dark and chilly. Jumping from the window looks good in films, but Teni was not too keen on doing anything heroic.

He made a face like a fried egg-plant, "And what if we break a few bones? I don't like all that *indralupta* ... that is, tomfoolery."

"Indralupta means baldness, not tomfoolery," said Kyabla.

Teni was even more furious. "Shut up. If I say indralupta means tomfoolery, then it does. Don't disturb me, Kyabla. I am trying to think out everything very clearly."

Kyabla made a face. "Then you sit here thinking. I am going to try and climb down the tree."

"This boy seems to be Poondicherry number one," said Teni. "Hey Pyala, you hold on to his legs tightly. If he falls down from the tree, we have had it."

I dived for Kyabla's feet. Kyabla rewarded me with a well-aimed kick.

I fell on Habul and he let out a shout. "I'm gone!"

"Quiet!" shouted Teni. "We are in grave danger. This is not the time to fight each other. Boys, please calm down and listen to me. The door is closed, let it be. We don't need to bother about that right now. Let us go back to our beds, under our blankets. In the morning, we can ..."

Teni was about to may much more, but terrible sounds came in from outside.

"Owls," said Habul.

The sounds appeared even more high-pitched.

"Owls do not sound like that," said Kyabla.

Suddenly, I knew what it was.

I, Pyalaram of Patoldanga, had suffered for years from fever. My spleen, which kept quiet as long as I lived on fish stew, now suddenly became jumpy. I could feel it trembling within me.

I climbed into a bed and drew the blanket over me.

"I have heard that sound before at my aunt's place in Gobardanga," I said. "That's the sound of babblers."

The sound continued outside.

Inside, Habul recited Jhumurlal's poem:

THE BABBLERS WILL SING IN CHORUS

AND MR. KUNDU MAKES HEADS DANCE

The birds went on for a few more minutes and then stopped.

By that time, my ears were ringing, my head was spinning, and my brain felt like a lump of overcooked *halwa* ...

Even our daredevil Kyabla was speechless. He no longer suggested climbing down the window.

Habul thought for a long time.

"So what are we going to do now?" he asked.

I wrapped the blanket even tighter around me. "If that sound starts again I'll surely have a heart attack."

Teni promptly rapped on my head. "You think a heart attack is funny? Failing in maths has really spoilt you. Just stay put, Pyala. We have enough problems as it is. If you try to have a heart attack, I'll give you one slap and your ears will land up in ..."

"Ernakulam," said Habul, forgetting for a moment that we were in an awful situation.

Kyabla looked grave. He had been quiet for a while.

"Tenida?" he said.

"Yes?"

"Can babblers sing in the night?"

"These are Kagamachi-special babblers," I said. "They can sing whenever they want."

Kyabla looked glum. "I have my doubts."

"What are your suspicions?"

"I think all this Kagamachi business is bogus. That green-bearded fellow is throwing red herrings at us. He is trying to frighten us at night. Whoever wears a green beard because he loves nature? And his formula has neither a head nor a tail to it. Theory of relativity and a digestive tonic? What does he think we are—people with zero IQ and upset tummies?"

"But what about that sly-looking fellow?" said Teni.

"And who took our pictures with a movie camera?" asked Habul.

"Who threw the crackers at us?" I asked.

"Hmm," said Kyabla. "I definitely heard the rustle of match boxes in his pocket. I think it was Sevenpenny who threw it at us in the fog and ..."

Kyabla had not quite finished when the terrible sound of the babbler's chorus started again.

"We're gone," said Habul.

I covered my ears with both hands.

Kyabla jumped up. "The sound is right beneath our window. Wait."

There was a jug full of water on the table. He picked it up and threw the water out of the window.

The chorus stopped midway. There was a sound of someone running away. And then, from very far, came a series of sneezes.

Kyabla laughed.

"See Tenida, those were not birds. That was a man. He has got a nice cold shower, he will sneeze the entire night now. He won't come to disturb us again."

"Poor Kagamachi. What if he gets pneumonia?" Habul asked.

"Let him die of pneumonia," said Teni. "How dare he keep us awake at night, showing films and making those awful sounds? Let's all hit our beds now. We will think of how to find a way out of all this tomorrow morning."

"Okay then, let's get some sleep," agreed Kyabla. "If the babblers come again, I will throw a chair at them."

We all climbed into our respective beds.

In five minutes, Teni's nose was singing, Habul and Kyabla also seemed quiet. But I lay wide awake.

The night was dense outside, crickets sang in the bushes. I could see the black tops of the hills and the stars shining like pinheads of light.

What if Kagamachi came again? I thought. He must surely be furious after getting drenched in cold water. There was no one to save us from him.

Habul was lying right beside me, but I needed to hear his voice. I gave him a gentle push.

"Hey Habul, are you sleeping?"

Habul gave out a tremendous yell and jumped up.

Teni stopped his snoring and shouted, "What's up?"

Kyabla tried to get down from his bed, blanket and all, and crashed onto the floor.

"What is it, Habul? Why are you shouting?" Teni asked.

"Kagamachi hit me."

I was about to say that it was me, not Kagamachi, when a dreadful thing happened.

We had put on the night lamp before going to bed. In its blue glow, we saw an awful sight.

In the middle of the room, a head was dancing. It had big teeth and two twinkling eyes. It was as if the head was laughing at us.

The four of us gave a big shout.

Instantly, the night lamp went out, someone laughed a terrible laugh and I ...

I fainted.

Just before fainting, I realised that I had fallen from the bed—like a ripe pumpkin—and was rolling on the floor.

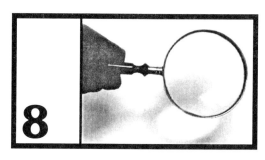

KAGAMACHI
LEAVES NO TRACE

I had fainted. Who could blame me? Could one keep one's senses intact if a head appeared and started dancing at the dead of the night?

But I wasn't even allowed to faint in peace. Someone gave my legs such a tug that I rolled on the floor, blanket and all.

I continued to keep my eyes tightly shut yelling, "Kagamachi!"

"Get up, or ..." shouted Kyabla.

I opened my eyes and sat up. There was no sign of the head.

The lights were on. Teni was staring upwards, open-mouthed. Habul was crawling out from beneath a bed.

"A ghost!" croaked Teni. "Kagamachi is nothing but a ghost."

Habul was shivering. "It stuck out its teeth in a ghastly grin. What if it had bitten one of us?"

"Hmm," said Kyabla.

"What, hmm?" I said. "I am leaving for Darjeeling tomorrow morning. As soon as it is light."

"Go wherever you want," replied Kyabla. "But look at the skylight once before you leave."

"Is the head coming again?" screamed Habul and disappeared under the bed.

Teni gave a jump and I climbed on a bed and pulled a blanket over my head.

Kyabla was very annoyed. "What cowards you are! Why don't you just look at the skylight once? It's open. If someone puts a head through that, and pulls it out again ..."

Teni said, "You mean that was a ..."

"Yes. It must have been a paper mask."

Habul had crept out once again.

"No, no," he protested. "It was not a mask. It had teeth this big ..."

"You shut up, Habul," said Kyabla. "Listen, if I don't grind those teeth to dust before I leave this place, my name is not Kushal Mitra."

"It will munch you up with those teeth, before you touch it." Habul was not to be outdone so easily.

Kyabla was about to grumble some more when the door opened and Sevenpenny Santra walked in.

"What's up?" he said. "It's half past twelve and you are still awake? I saw the light on in your room, so I came to see what the matter was."

Teni was furious. "Nice timing, I must say. We were nearly dead! The door was locked from outside while ghosts were dancing inside. How can we sleep through all that?"

"But the door was open," said Sevenpenny.

"No, Sir. We tried for half an hour."

Sevenpenny looked puzzled.

He drew a up chair and sat down. "Tell me what happened."

"We were shown a film for free," I said.

"The babblers sang till we were almost deaf. Kyabla stopped their racket with a jug of water."

"A head came down from the roof, bared all its teeth and danced around," said Habul.

Teni gritted his teeth. "That was a Mephistopheles, for sure. If I ever lay my hands on it, I'll give it one de la Grande and it will go yak yak."

"Wait, wait, let me see," said Sevenpenny. "And let me correct you before that. Mephistopheles means Satan. Masculine gender. In French, then, the adjective should be le Grande. That is, 'very large'. As for de ..."

"Stop, please stop," Teni said. "Here we are dying of our troubles, and you are giving us French lessons. What a man!"

"Alright, alright, forget it. Now tell me what happened."

"Didn't you hear the babblers?" I asked.

"Babblers?" Sevenpenny nearly went under, as if he was falling from the sky. "Of course not!"

"You must be a real Sleeping Beauty, then," said Habul. "The birds nearly turned us deaf, and you say you didn't even hear them?"

"Now, that's enough," interrupted Kyabla. "All of you are talking at once. How can he understand a thing?"

"Right. Order, order," said Teni.

Kyabla recounted the whole story in detail.

Sevenpenny's mouth fell open.

"My Gho ..." he said at least twice.

At the end of it, he sat there like a barn owl, staring at us with wide, round eyes.

"What do you make of it all?" asked Teni.

"It's Kagamachi again," moaned Sevenpenny. "Now he has attacked with his full force. I don't think I'll be able to save my formula any more. My years of research, my astounding discovery—all will be wasted."

"Why take all this trouble? Can't you call the police?"

"Police?" Sevenpenny Santra made a face, as if he had never heard a nastier word.

"Mr. Santra, what is in the room next to ours?" asked Kyabla.

"That?" said Sevenpenny. "That is a stockroom. All the excess furniture and broken knickknacks are stuffed there."

"How come its door has a square hole? A hole through which one can throw a projector picture on our walls?"

"A square hole?" Sevenpenny almost went under once again. "I don't know of any hole in any door."

"Then please be informed. Look at that."

Sevenpenny saw it, and sat down holding his head in his hands.

"Kagamachi right inside my house! Now I'm gone!" Grasping his green beard, he wept. "It's the end, the end."

"Let the end wait for a minute," said Kyabla. "Please open that door now."

"That door? That one can't be opened."

"Why?"

"I left its key behind in Calcutta. And as you can see, the door has two huge locks."

"Let's break them."

"You'll have to get a blacksmith from Darjeeling," said Sevenpenny.

"Let's have a look," said Teni.

We all went out. All the lights in the house were on. Sevenpenny must have put on all the switches.

But he was right about the locks. Nothing short of firing a cannon could break them.

"We must take a good look at them tomorrow morning," said Teni.

"Now let's have a look outside," said Kyabla.

I got a little scared. "Why outside? Who knows where Kagamachi's men are sitting, waiting for us. Besides, its freezing outside. Tomorrow we could ..."

Kyabla gave me a nasty look. "Why don't you go to bed, Pyala. We will go out."

What an idea! Alone in that room?

What if that head appeared once again? It wouldn't have to bite. Just another of those toothy smiles, and I would be past tense.

I scratched the top of my head.

"Okay, I'll come with you. I mean, it's my duty to encourage you all."

It was dark and cold outside. Pine trees stood shivering in the wind. Clouds had gathered on the tops of faraway hills. There was lightning in their midst. It was a night for curling up under the blanket after a nice dinner.

And here we were, roaming about in the cold. Damn Kagamachi ...

Sevenpenny had brought a torch. In its light, we saw a small puddle of water beneath our window. Near it were shoe marks.

"Water drove away the birds," said Kyabla.

We looked around for a few more minutes and then returned to the house.

"You people go to bed. I will stay awake and guard you all," offered Sevenpenny.

"We will also stay awake," said Teni.

"No, no. You are my guests, after all. Go on, I will call you if anything happens."

The wall clock struck one when we went to bed once again.

Kyabla did two things before he hit the bed.

First, he pulled the ropes to close all the skylights properly. Then he pushed the dressing table in front of the door of the next room, so that Kagamachi could not throw projector images on our walls once again.

We all fell asleep, thinking of Kagamachi.

We slept on till morning. But even in our dreams, we did not imagine the terrible things that awaited us the next day.

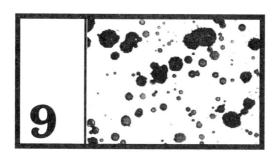

SEVENPENNY VANISHES

We were shaken out of our sleep by Kanchha's howls.

"What's up, Kanchha?"

"The master has vanished!"

"Where? How?"

Kanchha said a lot of things in Nepali. I don't think you will understand a word of it, so let me translate it for you.

What he said was: every day at five in the morning, Sevenpenny Santra used to have a cup of bad tea.

Bad tea? How could a man of such fine taste as Mr. Santra have bad tea?

"I think he means bed tea," Kyabla whispered in my ears.

Anyway, that morning Kanchha had entered Sevenpenny's room with a cup of tea.

He was dumbstruck by what he found there.

The room was ransacked. Pillows and blankets were strewn on the floor, a stool lay on its side. A broken hookah lay on the bed, a broom was flung outside the door and one dog-chewn sandal was on the stairs.

The only thing missing was Sevenpenny Santra. He had vanished into thin air.

The scene appeared to be straight out of a mystery novel.

"Maybe he has gone out for a walk," suggested Teni.

Kanchha vehemently denied that possibility.

For if Sevenpenny did not get his tea at five, he would call Kanchha at seven past five and shout "Gad, mad." That is, he would scold him in English. He never stepped out without his cup of tea.

Besides, no one saw him wrestling with his pillows and blankets. Above all, how could one explain the broken hookah, the broom, and the sandal?

In spite of his fright, Kanchha had searched for him everywhere. When he could not see even a hair of Sevenpenny's green beard, he came to wake us up.

For a few minutes, we stood there like fools.

"Let's have a look at the room," said Teni at last.

"What good would that do?" asked Habul. "Kagamachi has taken him away."

"Quiet, Habul," said Kyabla. "Why not take a look at the room once?"

We went to the room. Kanchha was right.

The room looked like a battlefield. Everything was strewn around. Broken hookah, torn sandal, broom: all were in place.

Teni frowned. He appeared to be giving the situation some deep thought.

"Kagamachi came wearing that chappal, smoking the hookah," he said finally.

"Right," said Habul. "And he had given Mr. Santra a good beating with that broom."

I had a brainwave.

"How can one smoke from a broken hookah? That hookah is a symbol. The Japanese write hookah poems, so he has left the hookah behind to tell us that he is a Japanese."

Kyabla made a face like a squashed poached egg.

"Pyala, stop showing off. The Japanese write Haiku poems, not hookah. And why should anyone put on seven-year-old dog-chewn sandals? And who ever has heard of a robber coming with a broom? They always bring pistols."

"Maybe Kagamachi is too poor to have a pistol. And how do you know that broom is just a broken broom? Maybe it has some horrible poison in every stick, maybe it has dynamite sticks hidden in it, maybe ..."

Kyabla's face changed to look like a plate of alu chaat.

"Maybe it has an atom bomb, two sputniks, twelve mice. All those three-penny detective novels have ruined your brains."

Before we could protest, he kicked the broom.

Nothing exploded, Kyabla was unharmed. The broom rolled down the steps and landed in the garden.

Just then, Kyabla cried: "Hey, what is this?"

A rolled-up paper was inserted into the narrow pipe of the hookah.

Habul picked up the hookah, Teni snatched the paper.

The four of us bent over it. The letter read:

"My dear four friends,

Kagamachi has surrounded the house with his gang. He will be here in two minutes. I know they will kidnap me, so I am writing this in a hurry. They will try to get the formula out of me. Please try to find me out, but beware, don't go to the police. If you do, they will immediately murder ..."

The letter ended here.

Sevenpenny had written it. There could not be any doubt about that. It was clear that Kagamachi's gang had caught him even as he was writing the letter.

The mystery was deep, the danger terrific.

The four of us scratched our heads. What now?

Teni spoke after a while. "Should we return to Darjeeling?"

"Not a bad idea," said Habul. "As soon as Bajra Bahadur comes with his car ..."

Kyabla was furious. "Aren't you ashamed of yourself? Mr. Santra invited us here to help him in his danger. And now you want to run away, leaving him in the hands of the gang? Are the boys of Patoldanga such cowards? How will you show your faces in Calcutta?"

Habul had one wonderful quality—he agreed with everyone.

"Yes, yes, you are right," he now said. "We won't be able to show our faces."

"But where will we find him? Perhaps they have hidden him in some secret vault ..."

"Secret vault?" Kyabla spluttered in rage. "You must be joking. Secret vaults are not so common, they are found only in detective novels. Come, let's search the pine forest behind the house. Then we will draw up a plan."

Teni scratched his head some more.

"You mean, now?"

"Right now."

Teni's long nose seemed to lose some of its height.

"I mean, shouldn't we have some tea before we go out? We have to keep up our strength, you know. Besides, I am also a little hungry ..."

"Is this the time to eat? Shame, shame."

That made Teni jump up. He drew himself up to his full height. He quickly did three sit-ups.

"All right, let's proceed," he said.

But that good boy, Kanchha, saved us. His master might be missing, but he had not forgotten his duty.

"Breakfast is ready. Please eat before you go out," he said.

We looked at Kyabla. Kyabla conceded.

"Okay, then, let's eat before we go. But mind you, we must be out in five minutes. Pyala can't sit here for half an hour, chewing on toast."

Why do they always blame me? I was hurt.

"And what about you? Didn't you chew on a chicken leg for full one hour yesterday?"

Teni gave my ears a hard pinch.

"Stop it, we shouldn't quarrel among ourselves at a time like this."

"What about Kyabla?" I cried.

"Right. He won't escape, either," said Teni, and swung his open hand towards Kyabla.

Kyabla ducked, and the slap landed on Habul's head.

"I'm gone! I'm gone," shouted Habul. He sounded exactly like an ox.

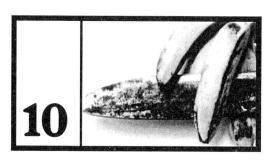

INSULT AND INJURY

After breakfast, we entered the pine forest.

The forest was right behind Jhow Bungalow. It stretched beyond the hilltop. Rows of pine trees, clumps of tiger fern, sehnai flowers and orchids surrounded us.

Groups of black and white swallows flew around. A black bird shot across our path like an arrow and disappeared amongst the bushes. The smell of wet earth, rocks, trees, rose together to overwhelm my senses.

I fell in love with the forest on that beautiful morning. I was ready to become a *sanyasi* if I could stay in that forest—of course, if food was taken care of.

I enjoyed the forest so much that I nearly forgot all about Sevenpenny Santra, Kagamachi and Kadamba Pakrashi.

I now understood why poems like 'O Pine' sprung up of their own in Sevenpenny's mind.

Even I could write a poem or two in a forest like this.

Teni spoilt my mood.

"This makes no sense," he said. "Where can we find him in this big forest? Besides, how do we know that they have hidden Sevenpenny here?"

"Right," I said. "Why should they take him through the forest instead of taking the road?"

"You want proof? Look at that." Kyabla pointed at a tangle of bushes.

Something shiny was stuck on a bush.

Habul caught it and brought it to us. It was a chocolate wrapper. That could only mean ...

"Kadamba Pakrashi," I said.

Habul began to search in the bush.

"Have you found anything else?" asked Kyabla.

"No, but I am looking," said Habul. "If the chocolate is also here, then we can enjoy a few bites."

"Come back, will you? Forget about chocolates," called out Kyabla.

Habul looked crestfallen.

Meanwhile, Teni had made another discovery.

Something was written in pencil, on the back of the chocolate wrapper.

A rhyme again!

Kyabla read it out:

Squadron leader Teni

Where is Sevenpenny?

Tee hee hee hee

What's hanging from the tree?

It had to be Kadamba Pakrashi, with his worn-out muffler and the sly smile.

"What do you think, Kyabla?" asked Teni.

"I think they are in this forest," Kyabla replied gravely.

But where in the forest?

"Should we go on walking in the forest till we cross the border and enter Sikkim?" I asked.

"Yes, if we need to." Kyabla appeared even more grave now.

"I'm gone," cried Habul.

Kyabla did not pay him any attention. He took out a piece of chewing gum from his pocket. Chewing on it slowly, he recited the lines of the rhyme.

"What does the last line mean? What can be hanging from the tree?" he mused.

"A jackfruit, perhaps?" said Habul.

"Really?" Teni brightened up. "Where? Where is it?"

"How can you find a jackfruit in a pine forest?" Kyabla flared up once again. "The talk of food makes you people mad. This must have a deeper meaning."

"What meaning?" said Teni, looking very disappointed.

"We must find out. Let's walk a little further."

We didn't have to go far. Again it was Habul who saw it.

"There! There it is," he shouted.

"What? Where?" We shouted even louder.

"On that tree. Can't you see?"

It was not a very tall tree. Long stick-like fruits hung from it, and a white bundle dangled from its topmost branch.

"That must be it," said Teni. "We must get it down."

"Let it be, Tenida," I pleaded. "Let hanging things hang on. Aren't we hung up enough already?"

"Yes, he's right," said Habul. "Who knows, there might be a bomb in that."

"Hmm," said Teni. "Not impossible."

"Cowards," said Kyabla. "You will never be able to deal with Kagamachi. Cover your faces and go back to Darjeeling."

The word, 'coward', always brought out the lion in Teni.

Even I, Pyalaram of Patoldanga, who can only have fish stew, felt something roar within me when I hear that word.

"What? You call me a coward? I'm climbing that tree right now. If we have to die, I must die first," cried Teni.

"Wait," I cried.

How could I pass on the chance to die like a hero? I stepped forward bravely.

"You are our leader, Tenida. Soldiers die before their captain does. I will climb the tree."

"Bravo," said Kyabla.

Habul and Teni clapped their hands.

Full of enthusiasm, I climbed up the tree.

Very soon I found out that there were worse things than laying down lives.

Red ants, for example.

"Go up!" cried Teni from beneath. "Think of yourself as the unconquerable, the unflinching hero."

It was definitely not the time for poetry. I made a face like a plate of upma and climbed to the top.

By the time I reached the white bundle, death by a bomb seemed far better than dying from ant bites.

"Get away!" I cried. "I'm dropping it."

I threw it down, then shut my eyes tightly.

There was no blast.

I opened my eyes and found the three figures moving close to the bundle. I climbed down the tree as fast as I could, before the ants could skin me alive.

I found my friends standing around the bundle, dumbstruck.

In it, there were four green bananas.

"What does this mean?" Teni was so puzzled that his long nose curled up like a *jalebi*. "Four bananas after all that trouble."

"Yes. And we are four. That means, one for each of us," explained Kyabla.

"That means we ..." began Habul.

He did not finish his sentence.

Chatang, chatang, chatang!

Hidden enemies were throwing missiles at us.

One hit Teni's nose, another hit Habul's head. Teni jumped up, crying "E ... e ... e ..."

"I'm gone, I'm gone," cried Habul.

He was right. He was quite gone. Two terrible missiles had hit Habul and Teni.

Rotten eggs!

Foul-smelling slime streaked down Teni's face and Habul's head.

I was about to say something when an egg hit my back. Another one went whizzing past Kyabla's ear, missing its target by an inch.

TWO+TWO=FOUR

The four bananas were bad enough, the rotten eggs had us flat on the ground.

Not that they hit us hard, but the smell! It was a miracle that none of us fainted right there.

"A nice job they have done! We must go and take a bath right away," said Habul.

"My new coat ..." I tried to pipe up.

Before we could finish, Kyabla cried out. "Tenida, look there!"

Teni was jumping around, shaking off the shells of the rotten egg.

"What now?" He stuck out all his teeth at Kyabla. "All this is your doing. That rascal Kagamachi ..."

"Look quickly, Tenida. Behind that tree."

He was right!

Someone was hiding behind the tree. He must have thrown the eggs at us.

How dare he do that?

Few people knew Teni like we did. He went around with us, making us buy him lots of aloo chaat, chops and cutlets, threatening to slap us hard if we dared protest.

But when it came to work, he was a different man. Then the leader in him came out.

Last year, there was a fire in a slum in our locality. Before the fire brigade could arrive, Teni had rescued a child from a burning hut.

Such is Teni, and that is why we love him so much.

The moment Teni caught sight of the enemy, he threw off his coat, let out a war cry and leapt after him.

"I will slap Kagamachi till his head flies off to Kathmandu!"

A loud cry of "De la Grande Mephistopheles" rent the forest sky as Teni shot after the man like an arrow.

We were too stunned even to say, "Yak Yak."

The man started running, too. I couldn't see him too well in the forest, but I had a feeling that I had seen him before.

In a minute, both had disappeared into the forest. We could only hear the sounds of their feet. Then there was the sound of a fall and a scuffle.

Teni called out loudly.

"Habul-Pyala-Kyabla! I've got him. Come quick!"

De la Grande Mephistopheles, yak yak!

The three of us ran after them.

The hilly road was uneven, full of loose pebbles. We slipped and fell. Some poisonous shrub made my right hand itch.

I fell several times, but we were beside Teni in a minute.

We found Teni sitting alone on the ground. He was holding a thick, brownish muffler in one hand and two chocolates in the other. Some papers lay strewn around him.

Before we could say anything, Teni spoke.

"I did catch him, but then I slipped on this wet stone. The man rolled off like a ripe pumpkin and escaped. I've twisted my leg, so I couldn't chase him."

"What are these?" asked Kyabla.

"These fell off Kagamachi's pocket. And I snatched off his muffler," said Teni.

Then he broke a piece from a chocolate and put it in his mouth.

"Wait a minute," said Kyabla. "Can't you recognise this muffler?"

"I won't even try," said Teni, relishing his chocolate. "It smells as bad as it looks. Kagamachi may be a famous scientist, but he has no taste, I must say."

"You don't understand," said Kyabla.

"And I don't want to," replied Teni. "Now please tie my twisted leg with the muffler."

It was Habul who first had the brainwave.

"Of course I know it. We saw it tied around Kadamba Pakrashi's neck."

"Yes, yes," I cried.

"Right! It escaped me so long," said Teni. "He was the man who gifted us a chocolate at Siliguri and then invited us to Jhow Bungalow. He is the chief assistant of Kagamachi, isn't he?"

Kyabla had picked up the papers lying on the ground.

I saw that both were printed handbills with the writing:

Soon to be printed

Famous mystery writer

Pundarik Kundu's Mystery Novel

Every page will make you shiver and tremble!

Publisher

Jagabandhu Chakladar and Co

13 Haran Jhampati Lane

Calcutta 72

As Habul, Kyabla and I tried to make sense of the handbills, Teni sucked at his chocolate as if nothing else mattered in the world.

Kyabla finished reading.

"What can this mean?" he wondered aloud.

Now was my turn. Kyabla never read detective novels. He always dismissed them as bogus. Habul cared only for cricket.

But I?

I don't let go a detective story. Ramhari Batabyal's "Bloody Bodies", "Scream of Skeletons" "Midnight's Vampires", Jadunandan Adhya's "Cobra's Tail", "Wasps and Weasels" "Headless in Darkness"—I have read them all.

Pundarik Kundu?

Yes, I had read his books too, but he was no match for Ramhari or Jadunandan. His "Bug in the Bed" was not too bad, though. Especially the place where detective Hirak Sen fits a microphone onto the murderer's bed. When the murderer talked in his sleep, the detective could hear all his words sitting two miles away.

"What does this mean? Who is Pundarik Kundu? And who is Jagabandhu Chakladar?"

"Pundarik Kundu is a writer of mystery thrillers," I said, "but his books do not sell well. And Jagabandhu Chakladar is his publisher."

Habul was looking at the muffler.

Suddenly he cried out in pain, threw the muffler to the ground and started shaking his hand.

"What's it Habul?" I cried. "Was there a poisonous injection inside the muffler?"

"What injection?" said Habul. "There was a red ant in that muffler. What a bite, my God!"

The injured ant was kicking its legs. Kyabla looked at it, then looked at my coat. He appeared deep in thought.

"Your coat also has a few red ants, Pyala," he said at last.

"Of course," I said. "I had a fight with them when I climbed up the tree."

"Hmm. Search the bushes around you. Can you see red ants?"

Teni spoke at last.

"Have you gone crazy, Kyabla? Have you stopped looking for Kagamachi to look for ants? Oh, if only I could catch that Kadamba ..."

"Kadamba will be caught soon. He cannot escape any more," said Kyabla. "Habul, Pyala, have you found any ants?"

"No, there are no red ants here," said Habul.

Just then, something fell off his coat. It was a broken shell from one of the rotten eggs. It was about to fly off in the wind, but Kyabla jumped up and caught it.

He looked at it closely, then wrapped it in his handkerchief and put it in his pocket.

"What's that, Kyabla?" said Teni. "Here we are dying of the smell of rotten eggs, and you are picking up shells?"

Kyabla did not reply to that.

"Tenida, can you get up?" he asked.

"I think so," he said. "The pain is better."

"Then let's go. Let's not delay things further."

"Go where?"

"To Jhow Bungalow. Right now."

"But what about Mr. Santra?" said Habul. "What if Kagamachi does something awful to him while we are gone?"

"Forget Kagamachi. Let's first get back to Jhow Bungalow. I've got a clue to this entire business. Only one thing still escapes me. If I can get that ..."

Just then, something came back to me. I had the hobby of collecting autographs of famous people.

About three years ago, I had gone to Pundarik Kundu's house at Salkia. He had been smoking a hookah. Somehow, I always thought detectives—and authors of detective stories—should smoke pipes like Sherlock Holmes. I didn't quite like Kundu's hookah. But now the scene came back to me and ...

A knot loosened and gave way in my head. I whispered into Kyabla's ears.

Kyabla jumped up three feet from the ground.

"Eureka, eureka!" he shouted.

"What is it?" Teni had come to a halt. "What have you found?"

"Everything," said Kyabla. "Two and two four, four and four eight. The equation is complete."

"What does that mean?"

"You'll know in fifteen minutes. But before that, we must congratulate Pyala. Reading detective fiction is not totally useless. As soon as we get back to Calcutta, I will treat him to hot cutlets from Chacha's hotel."

"Uh-uh," said Teni. "He won't be able to stand it. I'll have his share."

Habul nodded his head and said, "Right you are. I'll also help you. What do you say, Pyala?"

I made a face like *gajar halwa* and walked on.

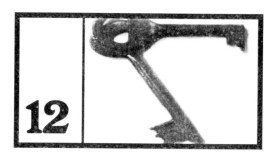

THE VILLAIN
IS UNMASKED

It happened just as we reached Jhow Bungalow.

Kanchha, who was doing some work in the front garden, caught sight of us. For a moment, he stood there, open-mouthed.

Then he ran inside.

"Why is Kanchha running away?" wondered Teni.

"He has not run away," said Kyabla. "He has gone to warn."

"Warn who?"

"Kagamachi."

Habul was startled. "What do you mean? Kanchha belongs to Kagamachi's gang?"

"Yes."

"Is Kagamachi hiding right here, in this house?" asked Teni.

Kyabla laughed. "Oh yes. Kagamachi and his entire troupe."

"Stop joking, Kyabla," Teni looked grave. "What if they attack us?"

"What do they have, except a broken hookah, a broom and a dog-chewn sandal? Surely we can resist them?"

We climbed the stairs to the first floor of Jhow Bungalow. There was no one to be seen anywhere. Even Kanchha had vanished.

Teni was limping, but had picked up a piece of wood on the way.

"Why the stick, Tenida?" I asked.

"We can fight the broom and the hookah with this."

"No need," said Kyabla. "I have a better weapon. Come with me ..."

Only Kyabla knew what he was up to.

I could guess some of it, but not all.

Our hearts thumping in our chests, we followed Kyabla. We had read enough mystery stories. We had had an adventure in a house in Ramgarh.

But this time, everything had fitted in too perfectly from the beginning.

And Sevenpenny ...

I had no doubt that Sevenpenny was the man.

"Here," said Kyabla.

We were standing in front of the stock room, with two locks hanging from its door.

"We must open this room," said Kyabla.

"How can we?" said Teni. "We'll have to bring an elephant to do the job."

Kyabla was desperate. "Let us push the door together. If the locks don't break, the door will."

"It would take the four of us four years," I thought, when Kanchha walked up to us.

"Should I make tea for you all?" he asked. His face looked perfectly innocent.

Kyabla turned to him. "We don't want tea," he said. "Bring the key to this room."

"Key?" Kanchha was startled. "What key? I don't know anything about any key."

Kyabla looked grave. "Don't lie, Kanchha. Lying is a sin. I know it is in your pocket. Take it out."

Kanchha looked a little bothered at the mention of sin.

He scratched his head for a while. "Yes, I have it with me. But the master has ordered me not to hand it to anyone."

"You must give it to us."

"I cannot." Kanchha stood firmly in his place.

"Tenida, Kanchha is a son of Nepal," said Kyabla. "He would rather die than disobey his master. So he won't give us the key. But we have to have it. So Teni, if your leg is not hurting too much ..."

Teni needed no more prompting.

With a cry of "De la Grande" he fell on Kanchha.

The next moment, a bunch of keys came out from Kanchha's pocket.

Kanchha was about to snatch it back. We would have had a scuffle right there.

But a rich, throaty voice came from somewhere.

"Kanchha, give them the keys. Don't resist."

Who said these words? We could not see anyone.

"Try the two long brass keys. That will save you the trouble of trying all of them." The voice boomed once again.

Now it was clear.

"Hey, that's Mr. Santra," said Habul.

Teni screwed up his nose. "It seems he is speaking from inside the room."

By that time, Kyabla had opened both locks and pushed the door open.

A stock room? Of course not.

It looked like a well-decorated house. There was a sofa, a clean mattress on the bed. A small projector stood in front of the door to our room.

And the man who was sitting on the sofa, staring right at us, was none other than Sevenpenny Santra.

"Hello, Pundarik Kundu. Take off your beard, please," said Kyabla.

Without a word, Sevenpenny took off his false green beard.

And I saw the man I had seen three years ago in Salkia, smoking a hookah.

"What is this?" Teni and Habul cried together.

"You'll get to know soon," said Kyabla. "Mr. Kundu?"

"Yes?"

"The man hiding behind your sofa, whose nose I saw a little while ago, that must be Jagabandhu Chakladar?"

Sevenpenny ... rather, Mr. Kundu, said, "Right. You are really bright. That's Jagabandhu."

"Why don't you ask him to come out?"

"Come out, Jagabandhu," requested Mr. Kundu.

Jagabandhu came out.

The same sly, foxy look, except the muffler. He looked at us, all innocence, as if he didn't know a thing.

"Come, come, sit down, all of you," said Sevenpenny. "Hey Kanchha, get some tea for all of us. Now tell us, how did you find out?"

"First, your poems and Kadamba Pakrashi's rhymes," explained Kyabla. "I had a feeling that they had something in common."

"Hmm. Then?"

"Second, your strange formula. You don't have a single book on science in your house. All you have are stacks of detective novels. Yet you call yourself a scientist. And how could you combine the theory of relativity with Aqua Tycotis? We are college students, after all. That is when I felt that you wanted to have some fun with us. Kagamachi was merely someone in your imagination."

"Go on."

"What else? What more should I say? You got Jagabandhu to take our picture at Sinchal, you showed us the film with the projector, made a paper mache head dance, got Jagabandhu to make the sound of babblers ..."

Jagabandhu spoke up at last.

"But how could you pour water on my head at midnight? Even now I have a headache, my nose is running."

"You are lucky we didn't drop a brick on your head," said Kyabla. "How could you wake us up at midnight? Now listen, Mr. Kundu: Tenida snatched away Jagabandhu's muffler. A red ant hidden in it bit Habul. It suddenly became clear to me that it was the man with the muffler who had climbed up the tree to tie the bundle of bananas. Then those rotten eggs. Look!" said Kyabla.

He took out the egg shell from his pocket.

"One can still read the number written on it with a violet pencil, 32. I had noticed earlier that the eggs in your kitchen are marked like this."

"Bravo," said Pundarik Kundu. "I write detective stories, but my detective Hirak Sen is no match for you people. But how did you know who I am?"

"Don't forget, you are an author," continued Kyabla. "Even if you put on a green beard, your fans will know you. Pyala here recognised you at once. And here is the handbill. It had fallen from Jagabandhu's pocket when Tenida attacked him. So now we know everything."

Pundarik and Jagabandhu sat there with glum faces.

"Why have you done all this to us?" Kyabla wanted to know.

Now Kundu laughed like a fox. "You understood all that, and can't you see this much? My books are not selling well. Jagabandhu and I were both feeling awful. I tried to copy from English novels, but found that Jadhunandar Adhya and Ramhari Batabyal have lifted all the plots. I came here to think of plots. Jagabandhu followed me here. He met you people on the way. He then had this brilliant idea: what if we make use of you and write a real detective story? Let me tell you something else. Poetry doesn't come to me easily. Jagabandhu may be a publisher, but he is a poet at heart. The poem 'O Pine' is his. He puzzled all of you with his rhymes, didn't he? The green beard was also his brain wave. We followed you to Tiger Hill and Sinchal. Jagabandhu took your pictures and threw the cracker. And then ... you know what happened then. But you have spoilt it all." Mr. Kundu let out a deep sigh. "If we had gone on with it, it would have made a terrific detective novel."

"And you could get Satyajit Ray to make a film out of it," said Kyabla. "But why did you throw all those rotten eggs? Can you imagine the condition of our clothes? Now who will pay the laundry charge?"

"I will." Mr. Kundu let out another sigh. "Jagabandhu, take out some chocolate. Maybe it will cheer us up a little."

"Chocolate? What chocolate? These boys have taken out whatever I had in my pocket," whined Jagabandhu.

And then?

Then Bajra Bahadur came with his car from Pubang. We all went for a visit to Pubang. He really took good care of us. We had a grand feast.

Then we returned to the Sanatorium in Darjeeling.

EPILOGUE:
PYALARAM'S REVENGE

One thing remains to be said: I could not let Pundarik Kundu get away with writing his detective story.

After all, he tried to fool us.

So here is my story.

I am publishing it before he can. If Kundu dares to write his book even after this, I'll sue him for stealing my story.

And all of you will be my witnesses, won't you?

Tara Publishing
Books with Perspective

Based in the Indian context, Tara books are original, enjoyable and contemporary. They range from novels, picture books and nonsense verse, to translations from Indian languages, gender and environment themes.

For ages 4 and above

- HenSparrow Turns Purple
- Monkey's Drum
- Tiger on a Tree
- The Fivetongued Firefanged Folkadotted Dragon Snake
- The Very Hungry Lion
- In the Dark
- Catch That Crocodile!

For ages 8 and above

- A Wild Elephant at Camp
- African Tales from Tendai's Grandmother
- Anything but a Grabooberry
- The Spectacular Spectacle Man
- Toys and Tales with Everyday Materials

For ages 10 and above

- Child Art with Everyday Materials
- Four Heroes and a Haunted House
- Landscapes: Children's Voices
- Leaf Life
- Puppets Unlimited with Everyday Materials
- The Mahabharatha (vols. I & II)
- Toys and Tales with Everyday Materials
- Trash! On Ragpicker Children and Recycling

For young adults

- Real Men Don't Pick Peonies (On an Alpine-style Ascent)

For adults/parents and educators

- Child Art with Everyday Materials
- Landscapes: Children's Voices
- Leaf Life
- Picturing Words & Reading Pictures
- Puppets Unlimited with Everyday Materials
- Toys and Tales with Everyday Materials
- Trash! On Ragpicker Children and Recycling

To know more about our titles, ask for our catalogue at:
TARA PUBLISHING
20/GA 'Shoreham'
5th Avenue, Besant Nagar
Chennai 600 090
tel: (044) 490 3318
fax: (044) 491 1788
e-mail: tara@vsnl.com